To Sophia & Cole,
Have a Blessed
Christmas!
Love,
Mrs. Scott

This Book Belongs To:

_____

_____

Tommy
NELSON

Merry Creature Christmas !

Merry Creature Christmas!

by **Dandi Daley Mackall**
Illustrations by **Gene Barretta**

Tommy NELSON®

www.tommynelson.com

A Division of Thomas Nelson, Inc.
www.ThomasNelson.com

Published in Nashville, Tennessee, by Tommy Nelson®, a Division of Thomas Nelson, Inc.

Library of Congress Cataloging-in-Publication Data

Mackall, Dandi Daley.
   Merry Creature Christmas! / by Dandi Daley Mackall ; illustrations by Gene Barretta.
      p. cm.
   Summary: Star, a wild colt living with the other animals in the deep forest, bravely wakes Big Bear from hibernation, and they all celebrate a Creature Christmas.
    ISBN 1-4003-0390-7 (picture book)
   [1. Christmas—Fiction. 2. Horses—Fiction. 3. Bears—Fiction. 4. Animals—Fiction. 5. Stories in rhyme.] I. Barretta, Gene, ill.
II. Title.
   PZ8.3.M179Me 2004
   [E]--dc22
                                    2003021835

04 05 06 07 08 LBK 5 4 3 2 1
Printed in the United States of America

Dedication

For Amy and Dee Ann, my "Merry" editors
~ Dandi

For my little brother, Billy.
We are blessed. Mom taught us to live each day like Christmas Day.
I love you.

Thanks to Charles M. Shulz and Bill Melendez for the choreography.
~ GB

In the forest deep, where the big bears sleep,
As the sun is setting, all the creatures creep.
Near the tallest tree, a nativity,
On the night of the Creature Christmas!

"Mustn't wake Big Bear!" says the forest mare,
When her colt, wild Star, rears and paws the air.
But that little Star wanders off too far
On the night of the Creature Christmas.

All the tiny mice, hanging streaks of ice,
Turn the prickly pine into a paradise,
While the porcupine pens a homemade sign
On the night of the Creature Christmas.

Star finds mistletoe as he sniffs the snow,
And he romps and he runs where no horse should go.
When he spots the cave, he thinks, *I'll be brave . . .*
On the night of the Creature Christmas!

Hear the owl exclaim—opossums do the same—
As that colt keeps going, thinking it's a game.
And they hear him neigh: "Bear! Come out and play
On the night of the Creature Christmas!"

In the cave, Big Bear, who is snoring there,
Knows it can't be springtime as he sniffs the air.
But he takes vacation from his hibernation
On the night of the Creature Christmas.

As the bear crawls out, all the creatures shout!
And they scamper and flutter and bound about!
With a smile so bright, and no trace of fright,
Little Star whinnies, "Merry Christmas!"

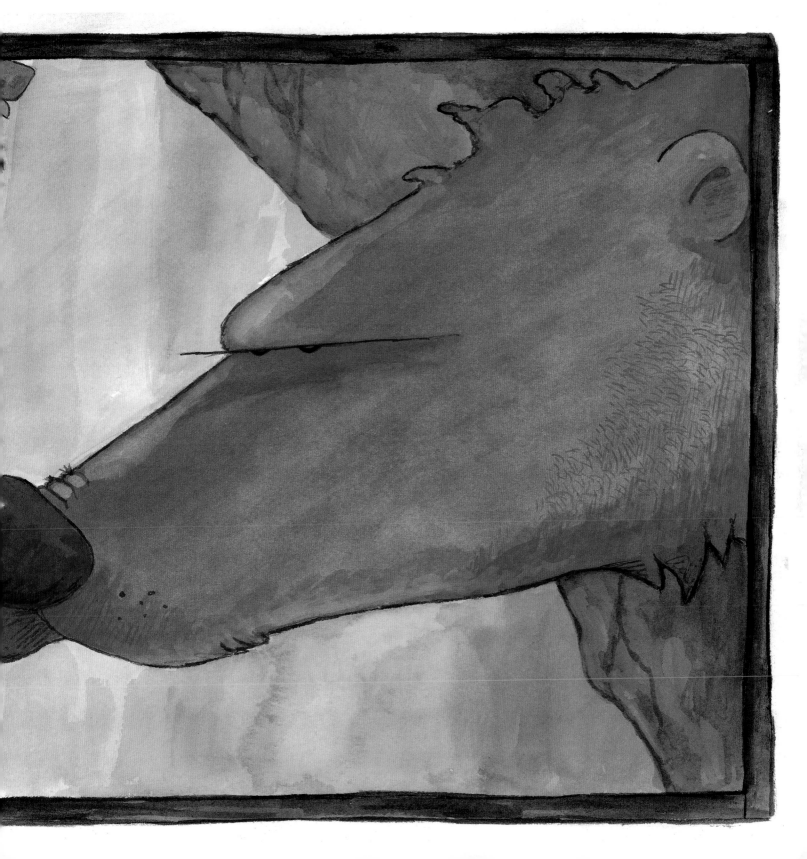

Charging on all fours, Big Bear growls and roars,
Frightening all the creatures in the great outdoors!

Then he rubs his eyes and says, to their surprise,
"Little Star, Merry Creature Christmas!"

Little Star, Big Bear, and the proud, white mare
Join the forest creatures dancing everywhere.
All the bluebirds sing, praising Christ the King,
On the night of the Creature Christmas.